THE ADVENTURES
OF
CAPTAIN Y

MICHELLE BLANCHE

To order additional copies of this book, contact:
Xlibris
844-714-8691
www.Xlibris.com
Orders@Xlibris.com

ISBN: Softcover   978-1-6698-4207-1
        EBook   978-1-6698-4206-4

Print information available on the last page

Rev. date: 08/08/2022

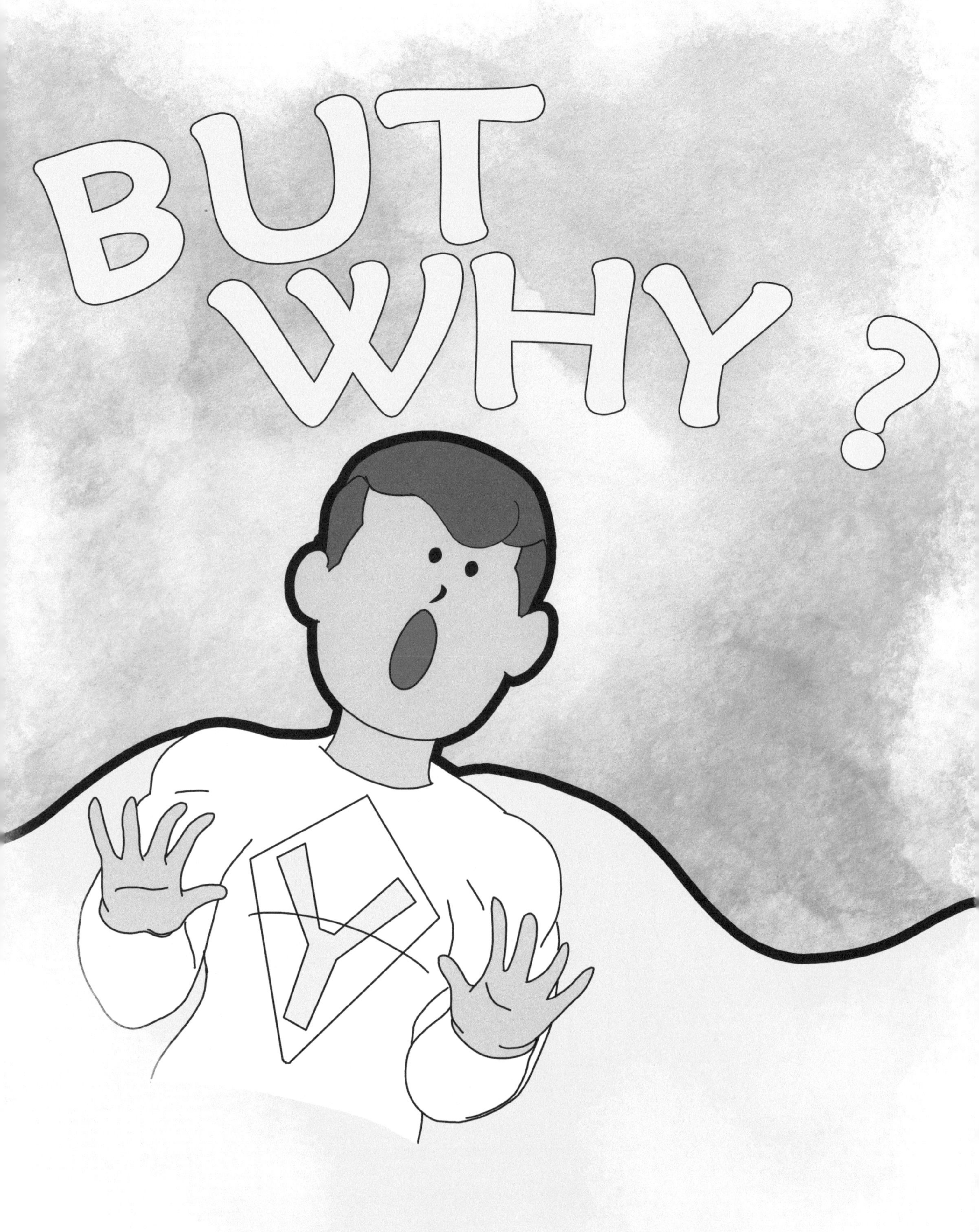
BUT WHY?

It was a busy day in the crowded town of Bigglesworth. People were scurrying about their daily lives.

In all the hustle and Bustle who would think that in a small bank, on a quiet cornet, Something devious would be taking place!

A masked man was holding up a bank while poor innocent people crouched down in fear!...

Suddenly out of no where-in crashed the most powerful hero of his Generation!

It was CAPTAIN Y!

I'm robbing this bank!
The Thug replied angrily.
BUT WHY?
Asked Captain Y.
?

Because I need LOTS AND LOTS OF MONEY! Replies the Crook.

"Because I spent all my money on video games! Now out of my way!

But **CAPTAIN Y** would not move out of his way. Instead, he moved in closer to the bad guy.

I'm going to steal all this money and there is nothing you can do to stop me CAPTAIN Y!

This started to make the bank robber a little crazy and He began to Loose it.

"Because you and all your silly questions can't stop me!" That's Why! Now I am leaving once and for all!

AAAAARghhh! Yelled the bank robber! No more Questions! You're driving me crazy!

Why? asked Captain Y

Because I don't Know Why! STOP Saying that!

Why? asked Captain Y

At this point the bank robber forgot about all his cash and just wanted to leave. He couldn't take anymore for **CAPTAIN Y'S** Question!

"Let me out!" He demanded.

"But why?" Asked **CAPTAIN Y.**

Because I just want to go home! Then the robber started to cry.

A few moments later the police arrived. They handcuffed the crook and thanked **CAPTAIN Y** for his services.

"Thank you again Captain Y." The officer smiled.

"No problem officer..." **CAPTAIN Y** replied.

With that, **CAPTAIN Y** Swooped up in the air and all was well in the crowded town of Bigglesworth.

THE END.

Printed in the United States
by Baker & Taylor Publisher Services